The Dead Sea Squirrels Series

Squirreled Away
Boy Meets Squirrels
Nutty Study Buddies
Squirrelnapped!

Coming Soon:
Tree-mendous Trouble
Whirly Squirrelies

Squirrelnapped!

Mike Nawrocki

Illustrated by Luke Séguin-Magee

Tyndale House Publishers, Inc.
Carol Stream, Illinois

Visit Tyndale's website for kids at www.tyndale.com/kids.

Visit the author's website at www.mikenawrocki.com.

TYNDALE is a registered trademark of Tyndale House Publishers, Inc. The Tyndale Kids logo is a trademark of Tyndale House Publishers, Inc.

The Dead Sea Squirrels is a registered trademark of Michael L. Nawrocki.

Squirrelnapped!

Designed by Libby Dykstra

Edited by Sarah Rubio

Published in association with the literary agency of Brentwood Studios, 1550 McEwen, Suite 300 PNB 17, Franklin, TN 37067.

Scripture quotations are taken from the *Holy Bible*, New Living Translation, copyright © 1996, 2004, 2015 by Tyndale House Foundation. Used by permission of Tyndale House Publishers, Inc., Carol Stream, Illinois 60188. All rights reserved.

Squirrelnapped! is a work of fiction. Where real people, events, establishments, organizations, or locales appear, they are used fictitiously. All other elements of the novel are drawn from the author's imagination.

For manufacturing information regarding this product, please call 1-800-323-9400.

For information about special discounts for bulk purchases, please contact Tyndale House Publishers at csresponse@tyndale.com, or call 1-800-323-9400.

Library of Congress Cataloging-in-Publication Data
Names: Nawrocki, Mike, author.
Title: Squirrelnapped! / Mike Nawrocki.
Description: Carol Stream, Illinois : Tyndale House Publishers, Inc., [2019]
| Series: The Dead Sea squirrels | Summary: When Pearl Squirrel is abducted, Michael's family bands together to rescue her, and the Squirrels teach Michael about honesty and responsibility by sharing stories of the Apostle Paul's life.
Identifiers: LCCN 2018050266 | ISBN 9781496435101 (sc)
Subjects: | CYAC: Conduct of life—Fiction. | Squirrels—Fiction. | Christian life—Fiction. | Family life—Fiction.
Classification: LCC PZ7.N185 Su 2019 | DDC [Fic]—dc23 LC record available at https://lccn.loc.gov/2018050266

Printed in the United States of America

25   24   23   22   21   20   19
7   6   5   4   3   2   1

To Justin—

For sticking closer than a brother to Michael and
for your contagious dedication to punctuality.
The best best friend ever.

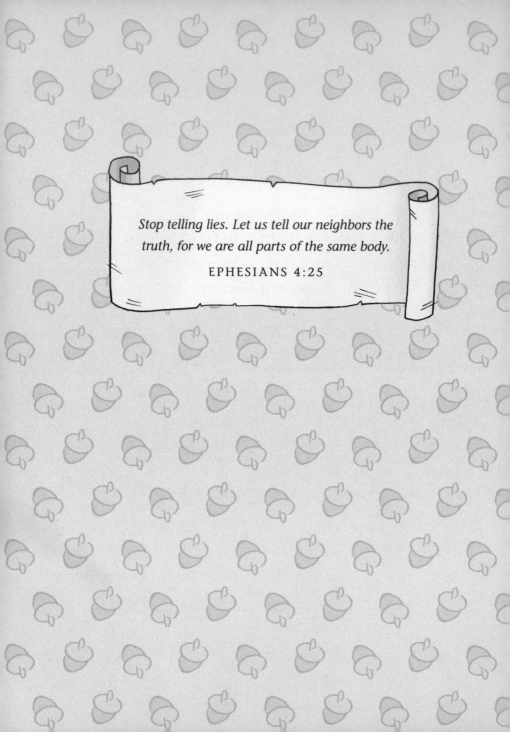

Stop telling lies. Let us tell our neighbors the truth, for we are all parts of the same body.

EPHESIANS 4:25

BUT WAIT!

BEFORE WE START...

Who are the Dead Sea Squirrels?

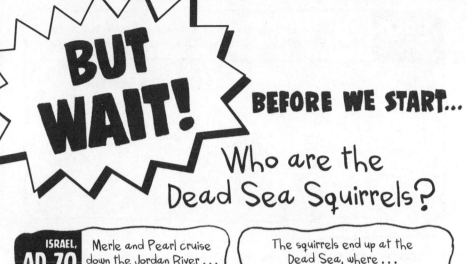

ISRAEL, AD 70

Merle and Pearl cruise down the Jordan River...

...on the vacation of a lifetime!

The squirrels end up at the Dead Sea, where...

You can't sink! I've always wanted to not sink!

Couldn't you have just worn your floaties in the lake back home?

Soon the two salty squirrels are hot, thirsty, and desperate for shade. Then they spot a cave.

If God wanted you to go into a cave, he would have made you a bat.

Merle's sense of adventure lures him into the cave, despite Pearl's protests.

1,950 YEARS LATER

Ten-year-old Michael Gomez is spending the summer at the Dead Sea with his professor dad and his best friend, Justin.

While exploring a cave (without his dad's permission), Michael discovers two dried-out, salt-covered critters and stashes them in his backpack.

Michael sneaks the squirrels back home with him to Tennessee.

He sets them up like posable action figures on his dresser—
under an open window.

While Michael is sleeping, a thunderstorm rolls in, and it begins to rain . . .

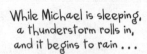

. . . rehydrating the squirrels!

Up and kicking again after almost 2,000 years, Merle and Pearl Squirrel have great stories and advice to share with the modern world.

They are the Dead Sea Squirrels!

CHAPTER 1

"Michael, can you please explain to me why you were dancing with squirrels?" Michael's mom stood just inside the door with her arms crossed. She'd been waiting for Michael to get home from the roller rink.

He was wearing his backpack, with Merle and Pearl Squirrel huddled quietly inside, listening through the canvas. Earlier that evening, Mrs. Gomez had entered Michael's room to discover him celebrating the almost-acing of his math test with Merle and Pearl. Pearl, who was quite the whiz with numbers, had tutored Michael for his test.

However, before Michael could offer an explanation to his shocked mother, Justin and Sadie had showed up to take Michael roller-skating. Now he was back home, and it was time to come clean.

"You promise not to tell Dad?" Michael asked timidly.

"I will do no such thing," Mrs. Gomez said. "You know they could have fleas?! I may have to fumigate your room."

"I do not have fl—"

Pearl cut off Merle's protest with a

paw over her husband's mouth. "Shhhhh, she'll hear you!"

"Well . . ." Michael hesitated. His dad finding out about the squirrels was Michael's biggest fear. If Dr. Gomez knew Michael had smuggled them home to Tennessee with him from the Dead Sea, he might make them go back—something neither Michael nor the squirrels wanted. "I was dancing with them because Pearl helped me pass my math test."

"Who is Pearl?" Mrs. Gomez questioned.

"One of the squirrels."

Mrs. Gomez raised her eyebrows. "A *squirrel* helped you with math?"

"Yup," Michael replied.

"Michael Karl Gomez," Michael's

mom began sternly, "if you expect me to believe for one mo—"

ZIIIIIP!

She stopped as the top of Michael's backpack unzipped itself.

Pearl popped her head out.

"AHHHHH!" Mrs. Gomez shouted.

"What are you doing?!" Michael tried to crane his head around to see.

"Please allow me to explain," Pearl said

calmly. Mrs. Gomez's face went as white as a sheet, and her knees weakened. Michael reached out to stop her from falling.

"Maybe you'd better sit down," Pearl offered. The squirrels and Michael then told her the whole story of how Merle and Pearl ended up in 21st-century Tennessee.

CHAPTER 2

Mrs. Gomez sat down on the living room couch. Michael sat next to her, and Merle and Pearl climbed out of Michael's backpack and perched on the ottoman while Pearl caught her up on the squirrels' adventures.

"Oh, my." Mrs. Gomez sighed. She turned to Michael. "You smuggled live animals out of a foreign country?"

"They weren't alive! Or at least I didn't think they were at the time," Michael answered.

"So you thought you were bringing DEAD animals home?"

"Um . . . yes?"

"WHY WOULD YOU DO THAT?!"
Mrs. Gomez demanded.

"Because . . . they were cool? They didn't stink or anything."

Michael's mom shook her head in disbelief.

"If I might add—" Merle interrupted—"we're very glad he did."

"Yes, we are," added Pearl. "Very thankful."

"And on top of it all, THEY TALK!" Mrs. Gomez cried.

"Not only that, but we're over 2,000 years old!" Merle pointed out proudly.

"Merle!" Pearl jabbed him with an elbow.

"Oh, my . . ." Mrs. Gomez repeated. She buried her face in her hands.

"That's why you can't tell Dad," Michael pleaded. "If he finds out, he might think he has no choice but to return Merle and Pearl to the Dead Sea."

"We don't want to go back!" Merle begged. "It's too dry, too hot, and waaaaay too salty!"

"We're not even from there!" Pearl put in.

Mrs. Gomez sat in silence for a few moments. "I dunno," she finally said.

"I don't feel right about not telling your father about this."

"Mom!" Michael protested. "Please?!"

"But it doesn't have to be right now. Dad is sleeping, and he needs to go in to work this weekend. I suppose it can wait until tomorrow night."

"But, Mom—"

"In the meantime," Mrs. Gomez continued, "I will help make Merle and Pearl feel at home and keep them safe from the cat. Have you met Mr. Nemesis yet?" she asked the squirrels.

"HAVE we?!" Pearl answered. "I don't think that cat likes us very much."

Merle sniffed. "Well, the feeling is mutual!"

CHAPTER 3

The first Saturday morning after the first full week of school is probably the best Saturday morning of the entire year. While your brain is adjusting to school time, your body is still on summer time, and after a few days of getting up early, nothing could be sweeter than sleeping in!

"Michael? Michael?!?!" Jane called out. Loudly.

Having a four-year-old sister can put a damper on your first-Saturday plans.

"Whaaaaat?" Michael groaned. He rolled over and opened his eyes just enough to see the clock on his nightstand. "Leave me alone. It's only eight o'clock."

Jane danced into his room. "Guess what?! I'm going to a birthday party!" she chirped.

"That's nice," Michael responded groggily. "Have fun."

"It's for Kennedy, and there's gonna be a piñata and a cake and a bouncy castle."

"MOOOOOM! Jane won't let me sleep!"

"C'mon, sweetie!" Mrs. Gomez called from the living room. "We've got to go. Let your brother sleep."

Jane didn't budge. "Guess what present I got her?"

"MOOOOOM!" Michael yelled out again.

"A Puny Puppy, with a windup bark. It's SO cute."

Michael pulled his pillow over his head. Jane finally got the hint and exited the room.

No sooner had Michael closed his eyes than he heard another familiar voice.

"So! What's the plan?" Merle asked

as he and Pearl bounced back into Michael's room through the open window, carrying armloads of acorns.

Michael, realizing he wasn't going to be doing any more sleeping on this first Saturday morning, rolled onto his back and opened his eyes. "You guys like soccer?" he asked.

"Can't say I've heard of it," Pearl responded.

Merle shook his head.

"Come with me." Michael got out of bed and grabbed his soccer ball from the closet. If anything was going to drag him out of bed on a first Saturday when he should be sleeping, it might as well be soccer. He walked down the hallway, past the closed door of Jane's room.

"Good morning, Mr. Nemesis!" Merle called through the door.

"Meowwwrrr," Mr. Nemesis replied grumpily.

Once in the living room, Michael began juggling the ball with his bare feet. He wasn't allowed to play soccer in the house, but with his dad at work and his mom and Jane on their way to a birthday party, he figured he could get away with it. Plus, he was still in his pajamas, so playing outside was not an option.

"Soccer is a game where you can't touch the ball

with your hands, so you have to be really good with your feet." Michael juggled the ball, getting 10 clean hits before it fell to the ground.

"Nice!" Merle commented. "But what if you have four paws?"

"Just use your bottom ones," Michael answered. Merle gave it a try. He got off a couple of hits before the ball sailed off his right paw and struck the side of the sofa. "Good try," Michael said. "Watch this!" He began juggling again, bouncing the ball high in the air.

Pearl glanced around the room, noting all the items that could potentially be damaged by a flying soccer ball. "Wouldn't it be better to do this outside?" she asked.

"You sound like my mom!" Michael laughed as he passed 15 hits. Feeling more confident, he bounced the ball higher. "My record is 50!"

"But don't you think you might—?"

Before Pearl could finish her thought, the ball bounced off the side of Michael's left foot and struck the top of his mom's prized ceramic elephant table. The table teetered over and fell onto the hard wood floor, followed by the lamp sitting on top of it.

The wooden lamp was unharmed, its shade bent slightly. But the elephant table was in about 100 pieces.

"Oh no!" Michael gasped.

"Is that bad?" Merle asked.

"It's worse than bad," Michael said.

And just like that, Michael had two large problems to deal with: his dad finding out about the squirrels and his mom finding out about her busted elephant. So much for a relaxing first Saturday.

CHAPTER 4

Eventually, most people, if they are
wise enough, learn that you
are better off dealing with
problems sooner rather
than later. A problem
hardly ever just goes
away. Even some kids
have learned this lesson.
Sadly, Michael was not
one of them. No sooner
had the broken pieces of
the elephant settled on
the floor than Michael
had collected them in a
box and moved them to
the garage workshop.

"Maybe Mom doesn't need to find out," Michael said.

"How could she not?" asked Merle. "This elephant is in a million pieces."

"Glue." Michael started pulling drawers open.

"What's glue?" Merle asked.

"Nothin'. What's glue with you?" Michael laughed.

Merle looked puzzled. "What's so funny?"

"Never mind. Just a silly joke. Glue is a sticky liquid that you can use to put things back together."

"Like sap?"

"Sap?" Michael said.

"Not much. What's sap with you?" Merle and Michael both laughed.

"That actually kind of works," Michael said.

"You two are hilarious." Pearl shook her head. "How is glue going to keep your mom from finding out you broke her elephant?"

"We'll glue it back together, and hopefully she won't be able to tell it was ever broken," Michael said. "She'll never need to know what happened."

Pearl frowned. "Like not telling your dad you smuggled two rodents out of Israel? I'm sensing a pattern here."

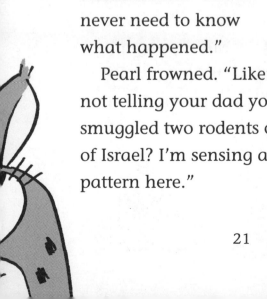

It took the better part of two hours, but with Merle's help, Michael was able to put the elephant back together, piece by piece. In the end, it *mostly* looked like an elephant, depending on where on an elephant you expected the trunk to be. Merle had become fascinated by glue during the process and had succeeded in creating a rather interesting sculpture out of items he found lying around the garage.

"Okay!" Michael dusted off his hands. "Help me put the elephant back, guys. Be careful, the glue isn't completely dry."

CHAPTER 5

"What is that hideous thing?" Mrs. Gomez asked as she came into the kitchen from the garage, carrying an armload of shopping bags. Jane skipped in behind her, holding a pink-and-green cupcake on a paper plate. Michael sat at the kitchen table, trying to act casual, as the squirrels hid on top of the cabinets.

"Umm . . ." Michael stammered. He realized he should have hidden Merle's experimental sculpture. "Just . . . stuff . . . with glue." Before his mom had a chance to ask any more questions, Michael changed the subject. "Thanks for bringing me a cupcake, Jane!"

"It's not for you," Jane said. "It's for Mr. Nemesis." She headed toward her bedroom to deliver her present to the cat.

"Where are the squirrels?" Mrs. Gomez whispered. Michael motioned to the cabinet above the countertop. Mrs. Gomez frowned and called out, "Jane, please don't let the cat out!"

"Why not?!" Jane complained from the living room.

"Just leave Mr. Nemesis in your room for now, please. You can give him the cupcake later," Mrs. Gomez said. She turned to Michael and the squirrels and smiled. "Look what I got!" She took a large box from one of the shopping bags. The box had a picture of a big hamster house. "And there's more in the car."

"Nice!" Michael said.

While Michael and the squirrels checked out Merle and Pearl's new house, Jane spotted the soccer ball next to a wall in the living room. She began to lightly tap it around with her feet, still holding the cupcake. She passed by the elephant table, which Michael had recently put back in place. He hadn't put the lamp back on it yet, knowing it probably couldn't take the weight until the glue

dried. The soccer ball rolled under the coffee table. Jane set the cupcake down on the elephant table. As she reached under the coffee table to grab the ball, the weight of the cupcake brought down the elephant.

CRASH!

CHAPTER 6

"Jane!!! What did you do?!" Mrs. Gomez
yelled as she ran out of the kitchen
toward the sound of clinking porcelain.
The elephant lay at Jane's feet in dozens
of pieces, the cupcake in the middle. The
soccer ball was in her hands.

"I . . . cupcake . . ." was all that Jane
could say.

"What?" Mrs. Gomez crossed her
arms. "You know not to play ball in
the house!"

Jane began to cry as Michael and
the squirrels peeked around the corner.
"The cupcake broke it!" she cried.

"Cupcakes do not smash tables!"
Mrs. Gomez said. "Why were you

playing ball in the living room?"

"But I just kicked it a little! I didn't hit the elephant," Jane cried.

Pearl nudged Michael. "Tell her," she whispered. "You're not going to let your little sister get in trouble for this, are you?"

Michael shrugged. This was going much better than he'd planned. "I dunno? Maybe?"

Pearl put her hands on her hips and glared at him.

"You go to your room right now, young lady. You need to think about obeying the rules and also about telling the truth." Mrs. Gomez pointed Jane toward her room.

Jane, still crying, went to her room. As she opened the door, Mr. Nemesis charged out and raced for the kitchen.

"Eeep!" Merle yelped as he and Pearl ducked behind Michael.

Mrs. Gomez grabbed the cat just before he made it into the kitchen. Mr. Nemesis squirmed and complained as she brought him back to Jane's room and closed the door.

"Your father brought that from Vietnam many years ago," Mrs. Gomez said sadly as she headed back to the scene of the crime.

Michael and the squirrels had come into the living room now that the coast was clear.

"Sorry, Mom," Michael said, half

sincerely. He could feel Pearl giving him the stink eye.

"It's not your fault," his mom said.

"Yes, it is," Pearl whispered.

"Shhhhh." Michael glared at her.

"Why don't you all set up Merle and Pearl's new house while I clean this up?" Mrs. Gomez said.

"That sounds wonderful," Pearl said. "And I can tell Michael a little story."

"Merle, do you remember when Paul was in jail?" Pearl asked her husband as they began unloading plastic tubes from the hamster-house boxes.

"Jail?!" Michael said. "Why are you bringing up jail?"

"Relax," Pearl said. "Nobody's going to jail over a broken elephant table."

"I dunno." Merle looked at them through a plastic tube. "People have gone for less."

31

"True," Pearl said. "The apostle Paul was sent to jail for preaching."

"Why would someone go to jail just for preaching?" Michael asked.

"The Romans thought the Good News that Paul was sharing stirred up too much trouble," Merle answered.

"Paul was sent to jail several times," Pearl continued. "He did a lot of writing there. In one letter, Paul wrote to a church he helped to start in Ephesus."

"Paul told the Ephesians—
that's what they call people from
Ephesus—about a great 'mys-
tery'—because of Jesus, they were
all now part of one big family,"
Merle added.

"And he told them how important it is for a family to tell the
truth to one another. Paul said,
'Stop telling lies. Let us tell our
neighbors the truth, for we are
all parts of the same body.'"

"But I didn't lie," Michael
insisted. "I just didn't tell Mom
what happened."

"That's the same thing as lying," Pearl said. "Telling the truth is about telling the whole story."

"Yep!" Merle nodded. "Not telling the whole story, exaggerating, cheating, not keeping your promises—all of that is being untruthful."

Michael had never thought about lying that way. He'd always thought lying was just saying something that he knew wasn't true. It was news to him that you could also lie by *not* saying something.

Pearl climbed up Michael's arm and sat on his shoulder. "When the people in God's family tell the truth to one another, it shows that we can count on one another, and it also shows people outside of our family the power of God's love in our lives!"

CHAPTER 8

"Can you hand me one of those curvy tubes?" Merle asked. The hamster house was starting to take shape. Pearl handed Merle a tube while Michael sat on the bed, thinking.

"But it's not like it makes that much difference if Mom knows I broke the elephant," Michael said.

"Hey, guys!" Justin burst through the door. "Your mom tells me—oh, cool!" Justin exclaimed as he noticed the hamster house.

Michael kept talking to Pearl. "Plus, it's no big deal for Jane to be grounded. She already went to the birthday party. Her favorite thing to do is stay in her

35

room and play with Mr. Nemesis, anyway."

"What are you talking about?" Justin asked.

But before Michael could answer, Mrs. Gomez entered the room.

"Oh, that's coming along really nicely!" Mrs. Gomez said, watching Merle snap two more tubes together. "You're very good with your paws, Merle!"

"Thank you!" Merle replied.

"So . . . I guess you filled your mom in on the squirrels?" Justin said.

"Yes," Mrs. Gomez said. "He told me last night, and we're going to tell his dad tonight, right, Michael?"

"Oh," Justin said, with a hint of fear in his voice.

"Yeah, I guess," Michael said.

"Is there anything else you'd like to share?" asked Pearl.

Michael glared at her. There was an awkward pause.

Finally, Justin broke the silence. "I . . . was actually wondering if you guys wanted to go to the park and play soccer?"

"Yes!" Michael said immediately. If he told his mom the truth about the table now, he would be grounded for sure. He needed to get out of the house as soon as possible.

"Oh, I love soccer!" Merle said.

"How do you know about soccer?" Justin asked.

"Come on! Let's go before it gets dark!" Michael grabbed his soccer ball and rushed out the door.

Justin looked after him, puzzled. "It's only noon."

CHAPTER 9

Michael and Justin raced their bikes to
the park. Merle and Pearl rode along
in their usual place inside Michael's
backpack, popping their heads out
of the top like puppies
hanging out a car
window, ears
flapping in
the wind.

"Woohoo!" Merle shouted. "This is even better than roller-skating!"

"I know, right?!" Michael called over his shoulder. He was relieved to be out of the house. He'd been starting to feel guilty; any longer and he might have had to come clean to his mom about Jane and the elephant.

They rolled up to the park to find
Sadie waiting for them. Before long,
a three-versus-two soccer game was
under way—Justin and Sadie against
Michael and the squirrels. Merle
turned out to be a natural. Squirrels'
ankle joints are super flex-
ible, which helps them
to climb up and
down trees, and had
the added benefit of
helping Merle con-
trol the ball amazingly
well. In no time, Michael
and the squirrels were up 5–0.

"This is not a fair match!" Sadie
complained.

Merle bicycle-kicked the ball into the
back of the net. "Where has this game
been all my life?!" he wondered aloud.

"Soccer's been around for thousands of years," Sadie informed Merle. "It was being played in China and parts of the Roman Empire in your day."

"If you wanna know anything about history," Michael said, "just ask Sadie."

"Yep! You don't know where you're going unless you know where you've been!" Sadie quoted. It sounded like something she had said many times before.

Pearl decided to sit out for a few minutes to rest and even up the teams. On

the sidelines, she noticed a nice, straight line of acorns running from the soccer field into a hedge of bushes. Due to her squirrel instincts, Pearl was always on the lookout for food, especially tasty acorns. Had she thought about it a little more, she might have noticed that they were laid out a little too neatly. When acorns fall naturally from oak trees, they don't land in a straight line.

"The Romans would wrap seeds or hair in linen cloth to make balls for kicking around," Pearl heard Sadie say in the distance as she collected the nuts, picking up the nicest ones as she followed the line into the hedge. As she crawled into the bushes, she suddenly

felt like she was walking on a wood floor. If she hadn't had her mind on collecting acorns, she might have thought this was a bit odd and turned around.

Suddenly, a door snapped shut behind Pearl. She was trapped in a cage!

CHAPTER 10

With Michael and Merle now up 12–0,
Justin was ready to call it quits. Sadie
was more than happy to keep relaying
the entire history of soccer to Merle,
but not surprisingly, teaching while
playing was not helping her team.

"I give up!" Justin said, huffing and
puffing. "You win, Michael and Merle.
Good game."

"I was just getting to the Middle
Ages," Sadie complained.

"Save it for the next time you're on
Michael's team," Justin said. "You guys
want to come back to my house for
some lemonade?"

Merle looked puzzled. "Lemonade?"

"It's a drink made out of lemons," Michael explained.

Merle's lips puckered, trying to imagine it.

"Not just lemons," Michael said. "It's got sugar, too."

Merle shrugged. "I'll give it a shot." He turned around, looking for Pearl. "Pearl! Time to go! Let's go get some lemon-made!"

"Lemon*ade*," Michael corrected.

"Lemon*ade*!" Merle called out. There was no answer.

"Where is she?" Sadie asked. Merle spotted a few acorns along the side-lines.

"Maybe she's collecting acorns," he said. "This way!" He followed the line of uncollected nuts into the hedge.

There was no sign of Pearl in the

bushes. Merle and the kids looked all around the park and into the woods.

"This is really odd," Merle said. "It isn't like Pearl at all to run off like that. It's a lot like me, but not like her."

Suddenly, a familiar voice rang out.

"Pearl!" Merle shouted. He and the kids raced back onto the field, toward Pearl's voice.

"Look!!!" Justin pointed at the parking lot.

Pearl turned and caught sight of them. "Help!!!" she called out again.

Merle looked up and could hardly believe his eyes. There was Pearl, trapped in a cage, being lowered into the trunk of a white Toyota by the man in the suit and sunglasses!

CHAPTER 11

Michael sprinted toward the bikes parked behind the soccer goals, Sadie and Justin close behind. "C'mon, Merle!" Michael shouted over his shoulder.

Merle just stood there for a moment, still in shock. But soon he shook it off and raced to catch up with the kids. If you've ever seen a squirrel crossing a street or running away from a dog, you know how fast they can be! Merle bounded into the backpack as Michael climbed up on his bike and began pedaling as fast as he could across the grass toward the parking lot.

"We're coming, Pearl!" Merle shouted. But now the trunk was closed, and there was no way of knowing if she could hear him.

The man in the suit and sunglasses revved up the car as the kids reached the edge of the parking lot on their bikes.

"Hey! What are you doing with our squirrel?!" Michael called out.

"Stop!" Justin shouted.

SCREEECH!!!

The tires of the car spun out on the blacktop, white smoke billowing out of the wheel wells.

"Can Toyotas do that?!" Justin wondered out loud. The car sped toward the road, leaving the kids struggling to keep up in its smoky trail.

"Pearl!" Merle screamed in his loudest squirrel voice.

Through the haze, Sadie was able to make out the license plate number. "CPG 872, CPG 872, CPG 872," she repeated.

Michael huffed as his legs spun faster than they ever had before. Finally, with the car around a corner and out of sight, he gave up and coasted down the street, struggling to catch his breath. "I can't keep up! I'm sorry, Merle. I'm sorry."

Merle said nothing as he gazed after the car.

"What are we gonna do?" Justin asked as he caught up with Michael.

"We need help." Michael turned and pedaled hard toward home, Justin and Sadie close behind him.

CHAPTER 12

Mrs. Gomez turned and smiled as Michael, Merle, Justin, and Sadie came bursting through Michael's bedroom door. She had been assembling Merle and Pearl's new house all afternoon and had just finished. The final result was a complicated network of plastic tubes, running wheels, and compartments of different sizes that took up almost half the room. Mrs. Gomez loved homemaking—even for squirrels. "Well? What do you—?"

"Mom! Someone kidnapped Pearl!" Michael shouted, interrupting her.

"I think the correct term would be *squirrelnapped*," Justin pointed out.

"That's not a thing," Sadie said.

"Well, she's not a kid."

"You don't have to be a kid to be kidna—"

"What happened?!" Mrs. Gomez asked, looking worried.

"This place is AMAZING!!!" Merle exclaimed, temporarily forgetting the matter at hand as he gazed upon the Taj Mahal of hamster/squirrel cages.

"Isn't it fun?" Mrs. Gomez replied, pleased by Merle's reaction.

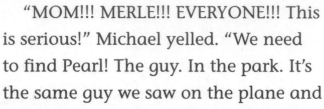

"MOM!!! MERLE!!! EVERYONE!!! This is serious!" Michael yelled. "We need to find Pearl! The guy. In the park. It's the same guy we saw on the plane and in the airport and at the roller rink. He must have been following us for a while."

"You saw him on the plane?" Mrs. Gomez frowned. "If he followed you over from Israel, we're going to need to let your father know right away."

"But he won't be home until later tonight!" Michael cried.

"We'll go tell him now," Mrs. Gomez replied. "If that man has ties to Israel, your dad needs to know right away. He may be a government agent."

*   *   *

"I thought I was grounded?" Jane asked as her mom strapped her into her car seat.

Justin and Sadie piled into the back on either side of her while Michael buckled up in front, with Merle tucked away in Michael's backpack at his feet.

"We're going to visit Daddy at work," Mrs. Gomez said.

Jane grinned. "Being grounded is fun!"

Justin and Sadie laughed.

"Why are you grounded?" Sadie asked Jane.

"I broke the elephant with a cupcake," Jane responded.

Had Michael bothered to turn around, he would have seen Justin and Sadie trade suspicious looks.

CHAPTER 13

"Professor? There are some people here to see you," announced Esteban through the speaker. Esteban was one of the students helping with Dr. Gomez's research.

Michael's dad was in a special lab, running a test on a series of scrolls to find out how old they were. "Who is it?" he asked, sounding surprised.

"Your whole family, plus a couple of other kids," Esteban said.

"Oh, great! Tell them I'll be right there, please."

*   *   *

"It's a little late for lunch, but it's good to see you!" Dr. Gomez said as he entered his office carrying a clipboard. He was wearing a white suit with a hood that made him look like a cross between an astronaut and a bee-keeper. "Something wrong?" he asked, noticing his wife and son's concerned expressions.

"Michael has something to tell you," Mrs. Gomez said.

"Okay," said Dr. Gomez. "What is it?"

Michael took a big gulp and looked up at his mom, then over at Justin and Sadie, before looking back to his dad. "Um . . . when we were at the Dead Sea this summer, I brought something home," he confessed. "Actually, two things."

"Really?" Mr. Gomez asked calmly. "What things did you bring back?"

Michael took off his backpack and

unzipped the top. He reached in and brought out Merle, who sat smiling sheepishly in Michael's palms.

At the sight of the small animal, Jane gasped with glee. "It's sooooo cute!!!"

Dr. Gomez's response was quite different. "You brought back a live

animal from another country?" he asked sternly.

Michael blushed and nodded.

"Well," Merle broke in, "I, for one, am certainly glad he did."

Dr. Gomez fainted dead away, his clipboard falling to the floor with a clunk.

"You seem to have that effect on people," Mrs. Gomez commented to Merle.

CHAPTER 14

With the help of a couple of cups of cold water, Dr. Gomez soon came to. Michael, Justin, and Merle then proceeded to fill him in on the whole story. Needless to say, he was not happy with Michael for keeping the squirrels a secret.

"Michael, withholding the truth is dishonest. We're a family, and we need to always tell each other the truth."

Michael thought his dad's words sounded awfully familiar. "I know, Dad. I'm sorry," he said. "I just thought they were so cool. I figured if I told you before we came home you wouldn't have let me bring them, and if I told you after, I'd get in trouble."

"Do you realize that not telling me may have gotten *Pearl* into trouble?" Dr. Gomez asked. "If I had known about the man in the suit and sunglasses sooner, I could have helped figure out why he is after the squirrels."

Michael hung his head. "Yes, sir."

"How do we find her now?" Merle asked.

"Sadie got the license plate number from the car," Justin said.

"CPG 872," Sadie repeated.

Dr. Gomez used one of the lab computers to track the license plate to a rental car agency in town. "It's a Frugal Rental, down by the airport," he said. "This is a long shot, but we might be able to track down the person who rented the car if we go to where the car was rented."

"Let's go!" Merle said urgently.

Jane stroked Merle's head with a finger. "Mommy, I think Mr. Nemesis would like the squirrel."

Merle laughed nervously. "Oh, I'm sure he would love me."

Mrs. Gomez went back home with Jane while Michael, Merle, Justin, and Sadie piled into Dr. Gomez's car and headed toward the airport.

CHAPTER 15

Dr. Gomez sped toward the airport.

"What do we do if the rental place won't tell us the man's name?" Sadie asked.

"They probably won't," Dr. Gomez said. "But we might be able to gather some clues there to help us find out who he is."

As Dr. Gomez exited the inter-state, Merle suddenly shouted, "Hold on!" He pointed. Along a frontage road sat a hotel with a few cars parked in the parking lot.

One of them was a white Toyota. "Isn't that the car?"

"That's a very popular car and a very popular color, but it can't hurt to take a closer look," Dr. Gomez said. He pulled around into the hotel parking lot and slowly rolled up to the back of the white car.

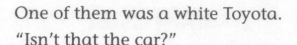

"CPG 872!" Sadie yelled.

"Well, what do you know?" Dr. Gomez said. "You just made our search a whole lot easier, Merle."

"It's the least I could do, considering Pearl's my wife," Merle answered.

Dr. Gomez parked, and the five of them crept toward the entrance of the hotel.

Before they even reached the reception desk, Michael spotted the man in the suit and sunglasses talking on his phone in the lobby. "That's him!" Michael whispered a little bit too loudly. Sunglasses Man started to turn around, and they all scrambled to take cover behind various chairs and potted plants. The man scanned the room and then turned back around, still talking on his phone.

Shhhhh!

Dr. Gomez shushed Michael as they poked their heads out from behind potted ferns on either side of the lobby entrance. "Let me hear what he's saying." The man was speaking in a language he probably thought no one in a hotel lobby in Tennessee would understand. He was mostly right—except Dr. Gomez understood Hebrew perfectly. After

72

a few moments, Dr. Gomez motioned for the kids and Merle to join him. They all slunk or scampered over to his giant fern.

"Okay, guys, listen," Dr. Gomez said seriously. "It sounds to me like this guy is a hired gun. He's working for an arti-fact collector. Black market tomb raider kind of stuff."

"Tomb raider?!" Michael whispered, alarmed.

"Yes, a tomb raider is someone who steals ancient artifacts," Dr. Gomez explained.

"Kind of like you did, Michael," Sadie joked.

"Hey, I'm no artifact!" Merle protested.

"Plus, they usually sell their stolen goods to collectors. That's what our squirrelnapper here is trying to do," Dr. Gomez continued. "Merle, you and Pearl would be extremely valuable to such a collector."

"I suppose two-thousand-year-old talking squirrels are fairly rare?" Merle said.

Dr. Gomez nodded. "That they are."

"Pearl must be in his hotel room, don't you think?" Sadie asked.

"I'm sure she is."

"How can we find out which one?" Justin asked.

Merle motioned toward the front desk. "Maybe we ask that guy?"

"No, he won't tell us," Dr. Gomez replied.

"Let's split up and look for her," Michael said. "We can each take a floor."

"I don't think so, Michael. This guy is dangerous."

"Which means Pearl is in danger!" Michael insisted. "We have to save her!"

Dr. Gomez sighed. "All right. I'll stay here in the lobby and keep an eye on him while you all spread out and look for Pearl. I'll come find you if he heads upstairs. Be careful!"

CHAPTER 16

Sadie started down the hall of the first floor while Michael and Justin took the elevator up to floors two and three. Merle headed outside to use his climbing skills to peek in windows.

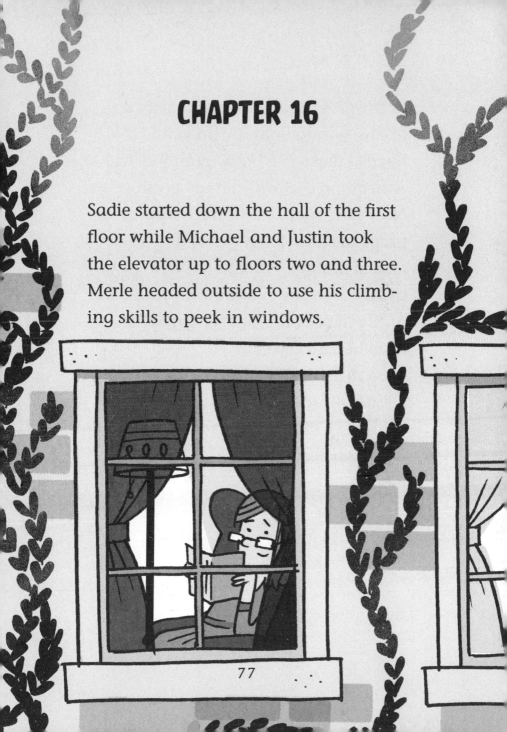

DING! The elevator door opened on the second floor. Justin exited and headed down the hallway to the left. A cleaning cart was parked outside one of the rooms, and the door was propped open. Justin peeked in and looked around. No sign of Pearl. Just then, a woman in a uniform with an armload of clean sheets popped up from behind the cart.

"AHHHHH!" Justin yelped.

"Hello!" the woman said cheerfully.

"Uh . . . hi," Justin said. "Umm . . . have you seen anything . . . suspicious today?"

"You mean besides you?" the woman asked with a smile. "No. Just another day at the office."

"Thanks." Justin continued down the hallway.

Meanwhile, Merle was busy outside, bounding from windowsill to windowsill. Since it was the middle of the day, most of the curtains were wide open, and Merle had no trouble peeking into the rooms. Not every room was empty, but there is nothing very alarming about seeing a squirrel on your windowsill. Unless you are a dog.

The Chihuahua was hardly any bigger than Merle, but it still surprised him and sent him springing backward into the branches of a nearby elm tree.

"Why you gotta scare me like that?!" Merle yelled at the dog. "I'm already having a bad day!"

"YAP YAP YAP!" the Chihuahua responded.

On the first floor, Sadie stopped a maintenance worker. "Did you happen to notice anybody carrying an animal in a small cage?"

"I haven't seen any cages, but someone's got a Chihuahua on the third floor," the man said. "I've been hearing that thing yapping off and on all day."

"Thanks." Sadie continued down the hall.

Up on the third floor, Michael pressed his ear to the door of room 302, listening for any sound that could be Pearl. Nothing. All he could hear was the barking of a small dog directly across the hall in room 303. As he turned to look, he caught sight of tag hanging from the door handle of room 317, near the very end of the hall. It was the only door on the floor with a *Do Not Disturb* sign. *Interesting,* Michael thought. He walked toward room 317 to investigate.

CHAPTER 17

Dr. Gomez sat in a deep, puffy lobby chair, pretending to read a complimentary *USA Today* while listening to the man in the suit and sunglasses carry on his conversation in Hebrew.

"Don't worry," the man said. "I'll have the other squirrel within 24 hours." After that the conversation got less interesting and soon came to an end. Then the man was quiet for a long time. Dr. Gomez lowered his newspaper slightly to take a peek at what he was up to. Not a good move. The man was looking right back at him! The man gave Dr. Gomez a suspicious glare, put his phone in his suit jacket pocket, and headed toward the elevators. Dr. Gomez waited for him to pass, then sprang up and ran for the stairs.

Sadie, wandering the first-floor halls, saw Dr. Gomez opening the stairway door. "What's up?" she whispered.

"He's going up!" Dr. Gomez sprinted up to the second floor.

"Oh no!" Sadie said helplessly, shaking her hands as she ran in place.

Dr. Gomez popped his head out of the doorway on the second floor to see Justin with his ear to the door of room 210. "Hide!" Dr. Gomez said, then zipped

back to the stairway to run up to the
third floor.

"Hide where?" Justin looked around
at all the closed and locked doors.

On the third floor, Dr. Gomez spotted Michael listening at the door of room 317.

DING! The elevator doors started to open!

Dr. Gomez waved frantically at Michael, signaling to him to hide.

Michael dove behind a cleaning cart parked outside of room 316. Dr. Gomez ducked back into the stairway just as

the man in the suit and sunglasses
stepped off the elevator and turned
toward Michael's hiding place!

CHAPTER 18

As Merle got close to the back of the
hotel, he spotted a window on the
third floor with the window cracked
open and the shades drawn. Most of
the windows he'd seen were closed
with the shades wide open.

What do we have here? Merle wondered. He bounced from windowsill
to tree branch to windowsill until he
reached the room near the very back.
Squirrels are quite agile and can fit
through very small openings, so Merle
had no problem squeezing in through
the cracked-open window. Once
inside the room, he poked his nose
though the curtains. It took his eyes

a moment to adjust to the darkened room, but soon he was able to make out a cage on top of a desk. Inside sat . . . Pearl! "PSSSSST! Pearl!" Merle whispered loudly.

"Merle!" Pearl jumped up. "You found me! Thank goodness!"

"It wasn't easy!" Merle said as he leaped over to the cage. "Actually, come to think of it, it wasn't that bad."

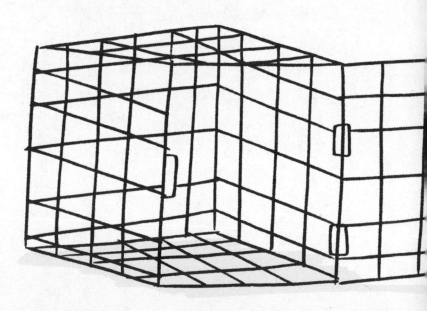

He unlatched the cage and swung the door open.

Pearl jumped into Merle's arms. "My hero!" she said. No sooner had the words left her mouth than the room door swung open—revealing the man in the suit and sunglasses! The next word out of Pearl's mouth was . . .

"AAAAAHHHHHHHHHH!!!"

In the hall, Michael recognized Pearl's scream and sprang into action! He jumped up and pushed the cleaning cart into the room.

As the man in the suit and sunglasses came toward the terrified squirrels, a cleaning cart appeared in the doorway behind him.

"AAAAAHHHHHHHHHH!!!" Michael yelled as he barreled the cart into the man's back, sending him flying facefirst onto the bed.

Thinking fast, Merle and Pearl jumped onto the cleaning cart and each grabbed a dirty sheet. With the speed of a spider wrapping a fly in silk, the two squirrels covered the squirrelnapper's head in used bedding.

"AAAAAHHHHHHHHHH!!!" yelled

the man in the suit, sunglasses, and
dirty-sheet helmet.

"Let's get out of here!" Merle yelled.
As the man struggled to free his head,
Merle and Pearl leaped out the window, and Michael took off running
down the hall toward the stairs.

CHAPTER 19

Pearl absolutely loved the new super-sized hamster home Mrs. Gomez had made for her and Merle. "This is just lovely, Mrs. Gomez!" Pearl marveled as everyone gathered in Michael's room (everyone except Mr. Nemesis, of course).

"I'm so happy you like it, Pearl. Welcome home!" Mrs. Gomez said.

"Yes. Welcome home," Merle repeated. "It's good to have you back. You had us worried there for a while."

"Believe me, I was worried too!" Pearl said. "Who is that man, and what does he want with Merle and me?"

"He wants to bring you back to the Dead Sea to sell you to a collector," Dr. Gomez said.

"We don't want to go back to the Dead Sea!" Merle pleaded.

"You know we're not even from there?" Pearl added. "It's no place for squirrels."

"It's too hot, too dry, and waaaaay too salty!" Merle added. "We like it much better here!"

"I'm sorry I didn't tell you about the squir-rels, Dad," Michael apologized. "I'm sorry, Pearl—if I would have let my dad know about you and Merle sooner, maybe you wouldn't have gotten into so much of a mess."

"Maybe not," Pearl said. "But it's always best to tell the whole story. The whole truth."

Michael nodded.

"Speaking of which . . ." Pearl looked at Michael.

Michael knew it was time to come clean. "Yeah, I know." He turned to his parents and sister. "Mom, Dad, Jane— I broke the elephant table. I was playing soccer in the house and accidentally knocked it over with the ball. I glued it back together, and it was still drying when Jane put her cupcake on it."

"My cupcake didn't break the elephant?" Jane asked, shocked.

"How could a cupcake break an elephant?" Dr. Gomez asked.

"I assumed Jane was playing with the ball in the house." Mrs. Gomez hugged Jane. "I'm sorry I didn't believe you, sweetie."

"Well, it was me playing ball in the house," Michael said. "I should have told you what really happened, but I didn't want to get in trouble."

"So you let your sister get in trouble instead?" Mrs. Gomez gave him a look.

"Yes, ma'am. I'm sorry, Jane. I'm sorry, Mom." Michael hung his head. "I'm grounded, right?"

"He's such a smart boy," Justin joked.

"Figured that one out all on his own." Sadie grinned.

Dr. Gomez laughed. "Right.

Grounded until further notice. It'll give you a chance to think about what can happen when you don't tell the whole truth."

"Yes, sir," Michael said.

"And we all need to think about how we're going to keep Pearl and Merle safe," Mrs. Gomez said. "Harboring two-thousand-year-old talking squirrels smuggled out of a foreign country is a big deal, and

we've got a lot to figure out. We've all got to watch our steps!"

Outside Michael's window, unseen by anyone in the room, a white Toyota rolled slowly down the street.

MICHAEL GOMEZ is an adventurous and active 10-year-old boy. He is kindhearted but often acts before he thinks. He's friendly and talkative and blissfully unaware that most of his classmates think he's a bit geeky. Michael is super excited to be in fifth grade, which, in his mind, makes him "grade school royalty!"

MERLE SQUIRREL may be thousands of years old, but he never really grew up. He has endless enthusiasm for anything new and interesting—especially this strange modern world he finds himself in. He marvels at the self-refilling bowl of fresh drinking water (otherwise known as a toilet) and supplements his regular diet of tree nuts with what he believes might be the world's most perfect food: chicken nuggets. He's old enough to know better, but he often finds it hard to do better. Good thing he's got his wife, Pearl, to help him make wise choices.

PEARL SQUIRREL is wise beyond her many, many, many years, with enough common sense for both her and Merle. When Michael's in a bind, she loves to share a lesson or bit of wisdom from Bible events she witnessed in her youth. Pearl's biggest quirk is that she is a nut hoarder. Having come from a world where food is scarce, her instinct is to grab whatever she can. The abundance and variety of nuts in present-day Tennessee can lead to distraction and storage issues.

JUSTIN KESSLER is Michael's best friend. Justin is quieter and has better judgment than Michael, and he is super smart. He's a rule follower and is obsessed with being on time. He'll usually give in to what Michael wants to do after warning him of the likely consequences.

SADIE HENDERSON is Michael and Justin's other best friend. She enjoys video games and bowling just as much as cheerleading and pajama parties. She gets mad respect from her classmates as the only kid at Walnut Creek Elementary who's not afraid of school bully Edgar. Though Sadie's in a different homeroom than her two best friends, the three always sit together at lunch and hang out after class.

DR. GOMEZ, a professor of anthropology, is not thrilled when he finds out that his son, Michael, smuggled two ancient squirrels home from their summer trip to the Dead Sea, but he ends up seeing great value in having them around as original sources for his research. Dad loves his son's adventurous spirit but wishes Michael would look (or at least peek) before he leaps.

MRS. GOMEZ teaches part-time at her daughter's preschool and is a full-time mom to Michael and Jane. She feels sorry for the fish-out-of-water squirrels and looks for ways to help them feel at home, including constructing and decorating an over-the-top hamster mansion for Merle and Pearl in Michael's room. She also can't help but call Michael by her favorite (and his least favorite) nickname, Cookies.

MR. NEMESIS is the Gomez family cat who becomes Merle and Pearl's true nemesis. Jealous of the time and attention given to the squirrels by his family, Mr. Nemesis is continuously coming up with brilliant and creative ways to get rid of them. He hides his ability to talk from the family, but not the squirrels.

JANE GOMEZ is Michael's little sister. She's super adorable but delights in getting her brother busted so she can be known as the "good child." She thinks Merle and Pearl are the cutest things she has ever seen in her whole life (next to Mr. Nemesis) and is fond of dressing them up in her doll clothes.

DR. GOMEZ'S
Historical Handbook

So now you've heard of the Dead Sea Squirrels, but what about the
DEAD SEA *SCROLLS*?

Way back in 1946, just after the end of World War II, in a cave along the banks of the Dead Sea, a 15-year-old boy came across some jars containing ancient scrolls while looking after his goats. When scholars and archaeologists found out about his discovery, the hunt for more scrolls was on! Over the next 10 years, many more scrolls and pieces of scrolls were found in 11 different caves.

There are different theories about exactly who wrote on the scrolls and hid them in the caves. One of the most popular ideas is that they belonged to a group of Jewish priests called Essenes, who lived in the desert because they had been thrown out of Jerusalem. One thing is for sure—the scrolls are very, very old! They were placed in the caves between the years 300 BC and AD 100!

Forty percent of the words on the scrolls come from the Bible. Parts of every Old Testament book except for the book of Esther have been discovered.

Of the remaining 60 percent, half are religious texts not found in the Bible, and half are historical records about the way people lived 2,000 years ago.

The discovery of the Dead Sea Scrolls is one of the most important archaeological finds in history!

About the Author

As co-creator of VeggieTales, co-founder
of Big Idea Entertainment, and the voice
of the beloved Larry the Cucumber,
MIKE NAWROCKI has been dedicated
to helping parents pass on biblical
values to their kids through storytelling
for over two decades. Mike currently
serves as Assistant Professor of Film and
Animation at Lipscomb University in
Nashville, Tennessee, and makes his
home in nearby Franklin with his wife,
Lisa, and their two children. The Dead
Sea Squirrels is Mike's first children's
book series.

See what's on the menu in
Tree-mendous Trouble!

...ng to
find out what happens to

THE
DEAD SEA
SQUIRRELS

Get the next book today!

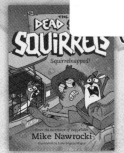

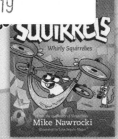

Watch out for more adventures with
Merle, Pearl, and all their friends!

CP1478